Little Red Snapperhood

Neal Gilbertsen   Illustrated by E von Zerbetz

a fishy
fairy tale

WestWinds Press®

Once upon a maritime,
So very long ago,
There lived a lovely snapper fish,
Who had a reddish glow.

With crimson cheeks and scarlet fins,
She clearly understood
Why other fish gave her the name
"Little Red Snapperhood."

One day her mother said to her,
"Oh dear, how time does fly!
Please rush to Grandma's distant home
This fresh-baked octopi."

LIST
• sea cucumber
• dogfish food
• pilotfish bread

SEA COW MILK

Red swam into a grove of kelp,
Where frightful creatures hide,
And soon a slimy wolf eel came
And slithered to her side.

"Where is it that you're going, girl?
What is that you've brought?
The fishing boats are out today.
Be careful! Don't get caught!"

"I'm going to my Grand-mama's,
And bringing octopi.
I shouldn't speak to strangers, sir,
So, thank you, and good-bye!"

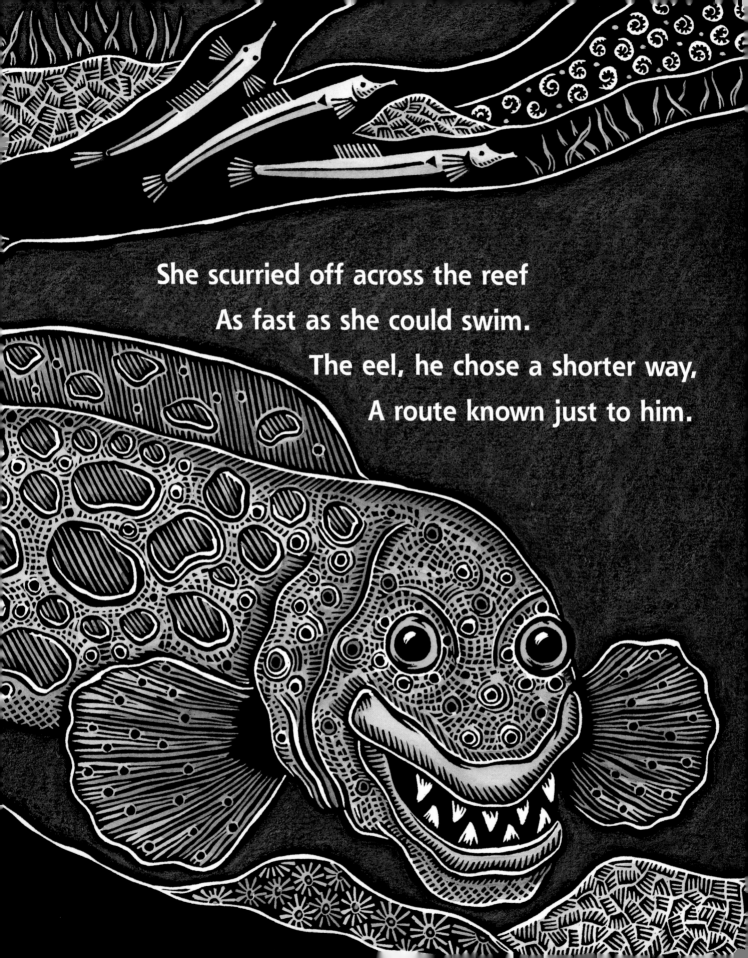

She scurried off across the reef
As fast as she could swim.
The eel, he chose a shorter way,
A route known just to him.

He got there first, and chased old Gram.
"Give me your oyster bed!"
He snuggled in and covered up
And took her place instead.

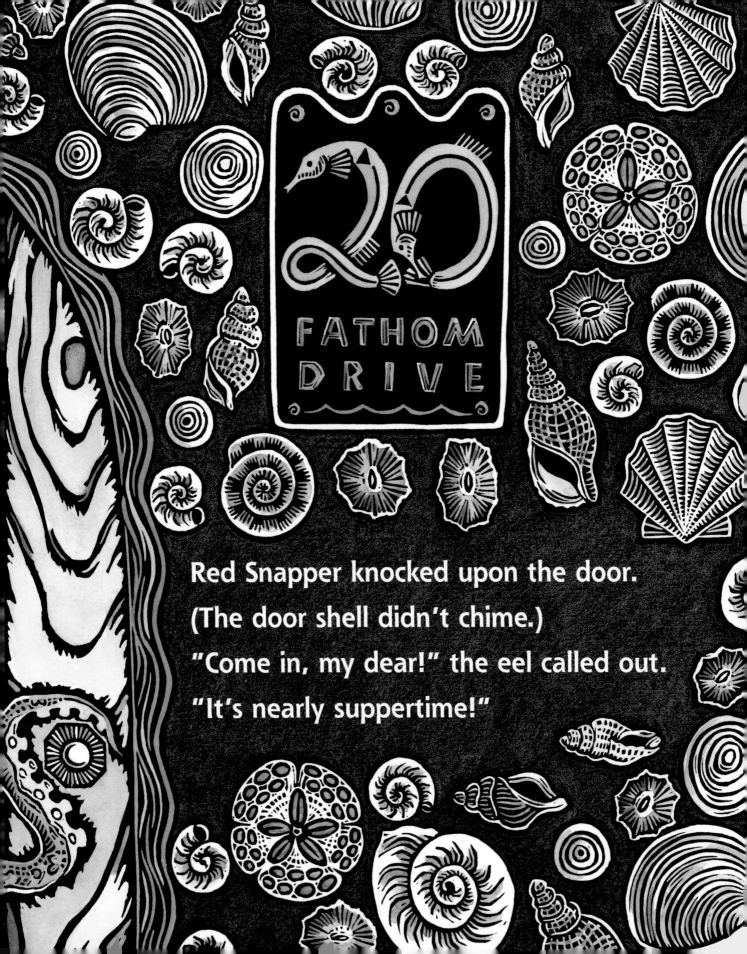

20
FATHOM
DRIVE

Red Snapper knocked upon the door.
(The door shell didn't chime.)
"Come in, my dear!" the eel called out.
"It's nearly suppertime!"

"Oh, Grandma, what big eyes you have!"

"To see you with, my dear."

"And what sharp teeth are in your mouth!"

"Come closer . . . over here . . . "

But Snapper sensed this wasn't Gram.
"I do not think I should."
Then Wolf Eel jumped from Grandma's bed
And caught her by the hood!

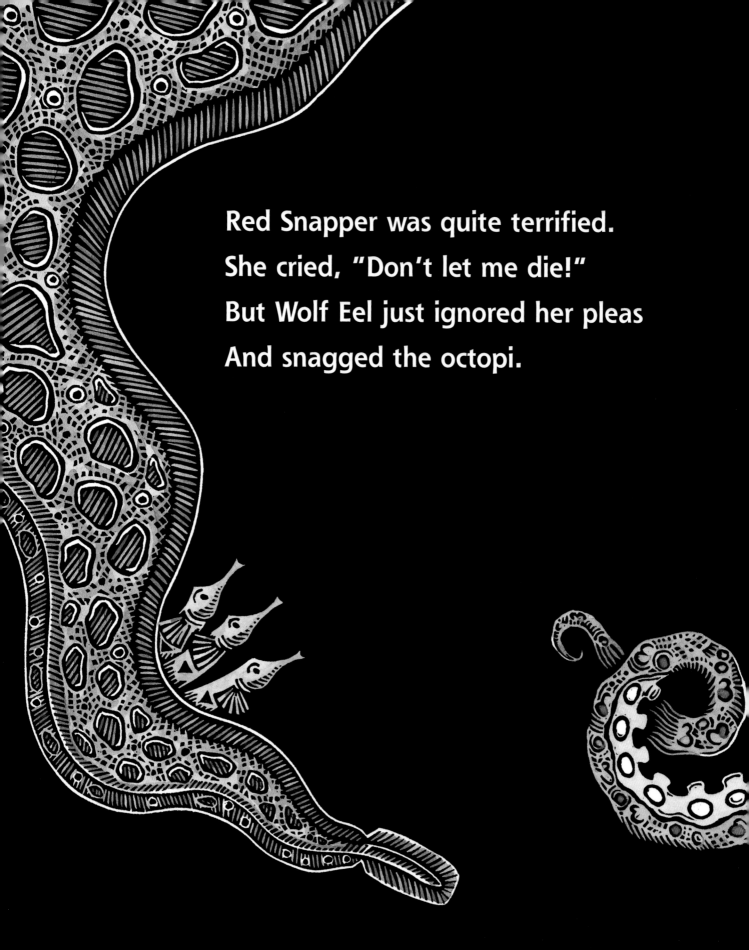

Red Snapper was quite terrified.
She cried, "Don't let me die!"
But Wolf Eel just ignored her pleas
And snagged the octopi.

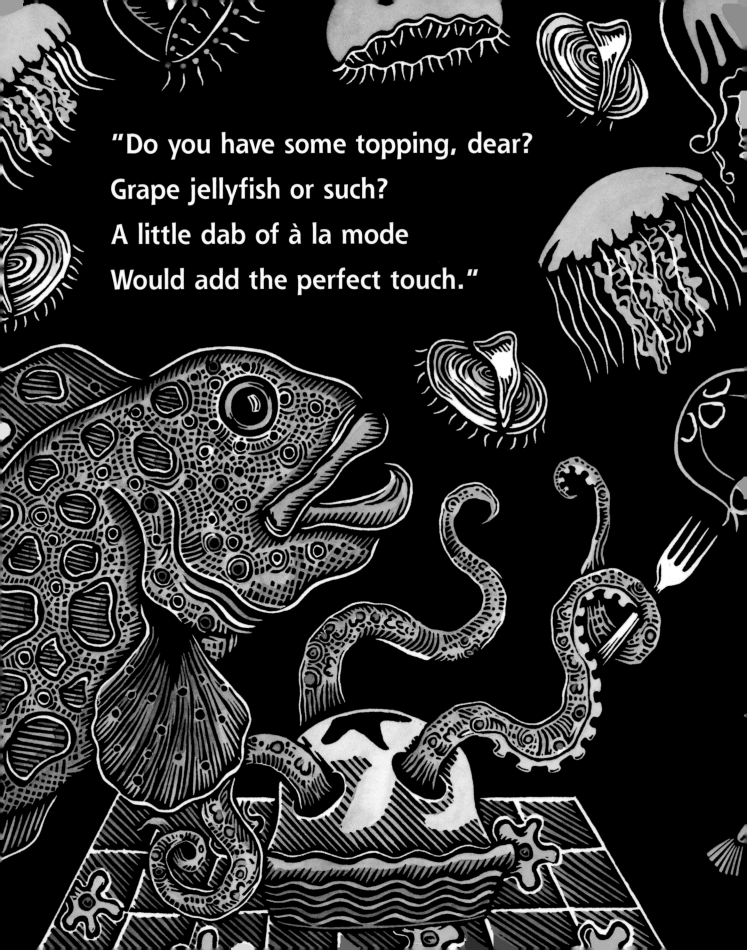

"Do you have some topping, dear?
Grape jellyfish or such?
A little dab of à la mode
Would add the perfect touch."

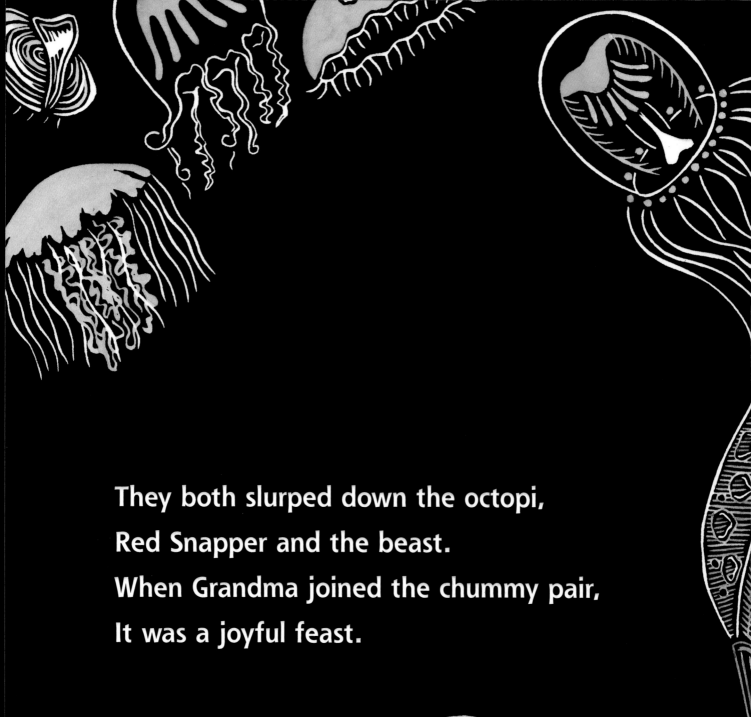

They both slurped down the octopi,

Red Snapper and the beast.

When Grandma joined the chummy pair,

It was a joyful feast.

And so, you see, my little fish,
Both ignorance and loathing
Can make us fear potential friends
Disguised in wolf-eel clothing.

For Deidra,
my true love, inspiration, and muse.
— N. G.

To the two G. Z.s: my father and my brother.
Remember the saltwater aquarium with the little rockfish!
— E. Z.

Text © 2003 by Neal Gilbertsen
Illustrations © 2003 by Evon Zerbetz

The artwork for this book is produced from linoleum blocks
that Evon carves and prints. She hand colors the finished linocut block prints.
Can you write your name backwards? Here is Evon's: *Evon Zerbetz*
All of the artwork for this book is carved in reverse—even the words
on the shopping list in the kitchen scene. LIST To find out more
about Evon's artwork, visit www.evonzerbetz.com.

Library of Congress Cataloguing-In-Publication Data
Gilbertsen, Neal W.
    Little Red Snapperhood : a fishy fairy tale / Neal Gilbertsen ; Evon Zerbetz, [ill.].
        p. cm.
    Summary: A rhyming, undersea adaptation of Little Red Riding Hood in which a little fish
    meets a wolf eel as she carries a baked octopi to her grandmother's house.
    ISBN 1-55868-683-5 — ISBN 1-55868-684-3 (softback)
    [1. Fairy tales.] I. Zerbetz, Evon, 1960– ill. II. Little Red Riding Hood English. III. Title.

PZ8.G375Li 2003
[398.2]
[E 2 21]   2002038341

President: Charles M. Hopkins
Associate Publisher: Douglas A. Pfeiffer
Editorial Staff: Timothy W. Frew, Tricia Brown, Jean Andrews,
Kathy Howard, Jean Bond-Slaughter
Production Staff: Richard L. Owsiany, Susan Dupere
Editor: Michelle McCann
Designer: Elizabeth Watson

WestWinds Press®
An imprint of Graphic Arts Center Publishing Company
P.O. Box 10306, Portland, Oregon 97296-0306
503-226-2402 / www.gacpc.com

Printed in Hong Kong